For Justine

Text copyright © 1994 by Random House, Inc. Illustrations copyright © 1994 by Jerry Smath. All rights reserved under International and Pan-American Copyright Conventions. Published in the United States by Random House, Inc., New York, and simultaneously in Canada by Random House of Canada Limited, Toronto.

Library of Congress Cataloging-in-Publication Data: Fisher, Maxine P. The country mouse & the city mouse : "Christmas is where the heart is" / by Maxine P. Fisher ; illustrated by Jerry Smath. p. cm. SUMMARY: Emily the country mouse leaves her home to visit her cousin Alexander in the city, but when a cat chases them they both return to the country for the kind of Christmas they really like. ISBN 0-679-84684-0 [1. Mice—Fiction. 2. Christmas—Fiction.] I. Smath, Jerry, ill. II. Title. III. Title: Country mouse and the city mouse. IV. Title: "Christmas is where the heart is." PZ7.F5346Co 1994 [E]—dc20 93-26488

Manufactured in the United States of America 10 9 8 7 6 5 4 3 2 1

The COUNTRY MOUSE and the City Mouse

by Maxine P. Fisher
illustrated by Jerry Smath

RANDOM HOUSE 🏠 NEW YORK

One crisp winter's day, the Johnson family was just sitting down to breakfast when they heard a horse neighing outside. Patty jumped up from the table and ran out. The mail had come at last!

"The mail! Oh boy, they're here!" she cried and hurried back inside. "Look, Dad. The Christmas catalog!"

"Goodness," said her father. "Is it that time already?"

At the mention of Christmas, Patty's younger brother, Kevin, scrambled down from his chair. In a moment, he was grabbing the catalog from Patty's hand. "Let me see!" he said eagerly.

"Kevin, take it easy!" Their mother laughed. "We all want to have a look."

Mother, Father, and Patty huddled over the catalog. Kevin couldn't see a thing.

Kevin wandered away, feeling just the tiniest bit sorry for himself. But passing the kitchen counter, he happened to spy a stray morsel of cheese. He took the cheese to the spot in the front hall where the floorboard had a hole in it. There he knelt and peered down, then let the chunk fall through the hole in the floor. "Your breakfast, Miss Mouse. See? I never forget you."

"Kevin!" called his mother. "Come back to the table. You haven't finished eating." Kevin returned to the table.

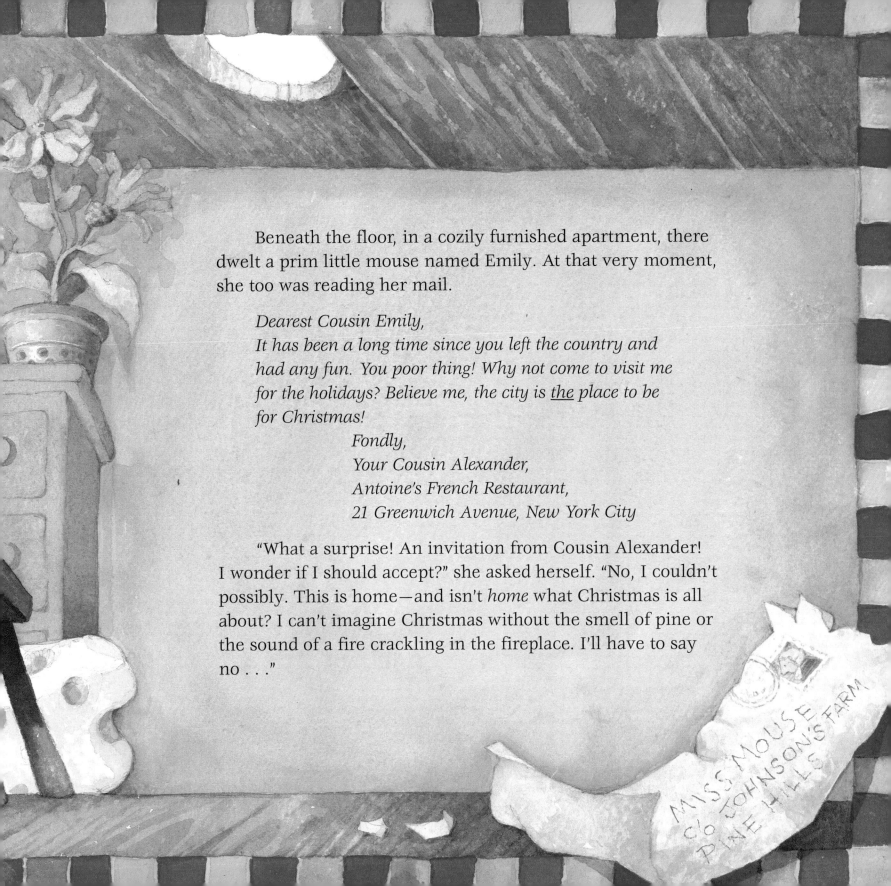

Beneath the floor, in a cozily furnished apartment, there dwelt a prim little mouse named Emily. At that very moment, she too was reading her mail.

Dearest Cousin Emily,
It has been a long time since you left the country and
had any fun. You poor thing! Why not come to visit me
for the holidays? Believe me, the city is <u>the</u> place to be
for Christmas!
         Fondly,
         Your Cousin Alexander,
         Antoine's French Restaurant,
         21 Greenwich Avenue, New York City

"What a surprise! An invitation from Cousin Alexander! I wonder if I should accept?" she asked herself. "No, I couldn't possibly. This is home—and isn't *home* what Christmas is all about? I can't imagine Christmas without the smell of pine or the sound of a fire crackling in the fireplace. I'll have to say no . . ."

MISS MOUSE
C/O JOHNSON'S FARM
PINE HILLS

Happy to have settled *that,* the mouse picked up her feather duster and started to clean. But suddenly she stopped. "On the other hand, it isn't every day one gets invited to the big city! It's bound to be exciting. And I haven't seen Cousin Alexander in such a long time. Perhaps I ought to go."

From under her bed, the little mouse drew out her old carpetbag. Now she was all for making the trip. But suddenly another worry struck her. "On the other hand, how could I leave Patty and Kevin for Christmas? Those children are like family to me! I couldn't bear to be away from them."

She pushed the bag back under the bed, glad to have made up her mind at last . . . when she had *another* thought. "On the other hand—goodness, there are so many hands— Alexander really *is* family. It's only natural to spend the holidays with him. That's it! I'll write him immediately and tell him I accept!"

And that is how, on the day before Christmas, Emily came to arrive at the train station in the city. My, what a big place! And so noisy and busy! How would she ever find her cousin? But Emily was a most optimistic mouse.

She set her bag on the platform and consulted her cousin's most recent letter. "Now let me see . . . Alexander said I should wait . . ."

Suddenly, out of the corner of her eye, she saw that her bag was about to be whisked away. "No! Stop! That's mine!" she called out in panic.

"Hush now! No need to get your tail in a tizzy, Emily. I was just going to help you with your bag!" said a very dapper-looking mouse.

"Alexander??? Oh, my! You look so elegant!"

"And you, my dear," her cousin replied, "look so . . . how shall I say? . . . healthy! Um . . . may I take your umbrella?"

The two cousins made their way through the station and out onto the streets, where crowds of people laden with boxes rushed to and fro. Horses whinnied, fire engines shrieked, and automobiles sent slush splattering onto the sidewalk. Emily could scarcely hear herself think.

"Is it always like this?" she shouted over the din.

"Oh, no!" Alexander shouted back. "It's quiet now. But you'll see. Things will perk up later on. Come on. Let's do the town!"

With that, he charged into the crowd. The country mouse darted after him, determined to keep him in view. But soon she found herself stopping to listen to a group of carolers. And when Emily next looked around, the city mouse had vanished.

She sat down and tried to think. A few steps away, a Santa began clanging his bell and shouting, "MER-RY CHRISTMAS, HO, HO, HO! MER-RY CHRISTMAS!!!"

Emily reached into her trusty bag and took out a map of the city. Now, if she could just find a quiet spot for a moment, surely she could locate Cousin Alexander's restaurant. Two stone lions loomed above her. They guarded the entrance to the city's great library. She climbed up onto the head of one and settled down with her map. "According to Alexander's letter, his restaurant should be right . . . here."

"Emily!" called out a familiar voice. "There you are! I was talking to you and suddenly—*poof!* You vanished!"

"Oh, Alexander! Thank goodness! I'm so glad to see you!"

At that moment, a trolley pulled up on the street below.
"There's our trolley, Emily. Let's make a dash for it!"

Down the library steps scampered the two mice.
"Wait . . ." gasped the country mouse. "Wait for me!"

Soon they were seated on the runner of a trolley, heading
downtown. The wind brushed their faces, and the Christmas
lights blazed by. At the last stop they jumped off.

"Only a block or two more," said Alexander, racing ahead.

"Why is everyone here always rushing?" panted Emily.

At last, Alexander stopped. "Here we are!" he said
proudly. "Antoine's. The best French restaurant in all New
York!"

"Oh, Alexander, it's even more beautiful than I imagined!"
Emily exclaimed.

"And just wait until you sample the food! *C'est vraiment
marvelouuuus!*"

The two mice skipped through the restaurant. As they passed the kitchen, Alexander pointed out a man wearing a tall, funny white hat and whispered, "Now you must be quiet, Emily. Monsieur LeChef does not like mice."

Around the next corner was Alexander's home. Emily gasped. Never had she seen such luxury. Such furnishings! Compared to her humble country home, this was truly a palace.

"I'm not used to anything this grand!" she exclaimed.

Alexander disappeared. A few moments later, he returned with a tray piled high.

"For Madame's pleasure. The very best from Antoine's kitchen."

Emily nearly swooned. "*Mmmm!* It smells heavenly. But what exactly is all of this?"

"Ah, for the cheeses: we have the Roquefort, Camembert, and Brie. Then here we have *andouillettes, saucissons, pâté de foie gras,* and for the desserts . . ."

Emily laughed. "Stop! I'll never remember all those names."

Emily took a bite of something. The taste was delightful. "*Saucisson!*" said Alexander.

"Sounds like music, but it tastes like sausage!"

The two mice laughed. Then Emily remembered something. "Oh, Alexander, before I forget, I've brought you a small gift for Christmas."

Emily took out a small wrapped package.

"Why, Emily, thank you!"

When Alexander opened the box, he found a pair of bright green and yellow knitted socks.

"I made them myself!" said Emily.

Her cousin did not know what to say. He didn't want to sound ungrateful. But they were not exactly his taste. "They are . . . how shall I say . . . extraordinary!" he said at last. "And I have a little something for you."

"Oh, Alexander! It's beautiful!" said Emily as she gazed on a painted paper fan. To Emily it was a treasure, though not exactly useful.

"I'm glad you like it," said Alexander, looking pleased.

That night, the country mouse lay awake while Alexander was already snoring. How can he go to sleep after so much rich food? Emily wondered. It *was* good, though, she thought. Yes, Alexander was right. This is the place to be for the holidays. But I do miss the pine forest and my spot by the fireplace. And I miss the children most of all. She yawned. And the next moment, she too was fast asleep.

Back at the farmhouse, the two children were peering down the hole in the floorboard.

"Where do you suppose she went?" Patty asked, worried.

"I don't know," Kevin answered. "But I hope she comes back."

"I'm sure she will," his sister said quietly.

That year, Monsieur LeChef received a special Christmas gift from his wife: a kitten named Miou-Miou. On Christmas morning, Monsieur and Miou-Miou were having a little chat in the kitchen.

"Now, Miou-Miou, my sweet Christmas kitty," began Monsieur LeChef, "*this* is where you will work. Yes. Your job is to find those nasty, naughty little beasties who steal my *andouillettes* and *fromage*, who ruin my *tartes* by nibbling away at the crust, who dive into my *mousse au chocolat* as if into a swimming pool. Oooh, I hate them so. But their days are numbered. It's war!"

Only a few feet away, the cousins were waking. "*Mmmm!*" said Emily, stretching. "Something smells wonderful!"

"Monsieur LeChef is preparing his holiday menu. Let me guess. *Coquilles St. Jacques.* That's scallops baked with butter and breadcrumbs, then sautéed with onions, prawns, wine, and a cream sauce. Oh! Come! I'll show you around the kitchen!"

In a flash, they were up and out and onto the counter, amongst all the yummy ingredients. "Ah, peaches!" exclaimed Alexander. "I see we are having *pêches cardinal* for dessert. That's poached peaches with a raspberry purée. *Mmm . . .* confectioners' sugar. Monsieur will use it for the *crème Chantilly*. He will beat it with cream and raspberries with that thing just behind you."

Emily turned and bumped into the eggbeater. It started to topple down. She squealed in fright. But Alexander pulled her away just as she was about to be crushed. "Shh! . . . Let me help you." Before he could say another word, Miou-Miou was flying toward them.

Alexander froze. Luckily, Emily had her wits about her. She grabbed her cousin just as the monster was about to pounce on them. "Quick, this way!" urged Emily.

The two darted behind the stove, but suddenly they heard a loud SNAP! "What was that?" asked Emily, terrified.

"A mousetrap! I can't believe it. It's a declaration of war!"

"Oh, what shall we do?"

The cat screamed, and the chef came running into the kitchen. "Oooh, *two* naughty mousies! Good kitty-cat!"

Monsieur LeChef, broom in hand, was now heading at full speed for the mice's hideout. "We've got to make a run for it!" cried Alexander. "It's our only chance. Follow me."

Zigzagging across the floor, they raced, trying to throw the tiger off their trail. All around them, they heard the sounds of traps snapping and the broom thwacking as again and again the chef brought it down upon the floor.

The two mice sped out of the kitchen, past the dining room, out of the restaurant, and onto the street. On and on they ran, their hearts pounding, until, exhausted, they collapsed on the sidewalk. "It's not exactly the Christmas I promised you, Emily, is it?" said Alexander after he had finally caught his breath.

"Well, you *did* say it would be exciting!"

"Yes, but I didn't mean *this* exciting."

Suddenly, Emily sniffed the air. She smelled something familiar. Something wonderful! "What is it, Emily?" her cousin asked.

"Pine. I smell pine trees!"

Emily was right, of course. For there on the curb lay a pile of unsold Christmas trees. She sighed. "Back home, the pine trees stand straight up and look into the sky. Oh, I do prefer seeing them that way."

"I'm sorry your Christmas is ruined, Emily," Alexander said sadly.

"But Christmas isn't over yet," said Emily. "And these trees have given me an idea. Why don't you come home with me and spend Christmas in the country? There's still time if we hurry!"

Ordinarily, Alexander never left the city. But this time he found it a splendid idea. "I would enjoy that, Emily."

So the two mice set off for the train station and the long ride to the country and the farmhouse Emily called home.

When they finally arrived outside the hole in the floorboard, she paused and cried out in delight. For there awaiting them was a tiny Christmas tree and two small boxes wrapped in colored foil. Beside them were dollhouse-size plates piled with turkey, stuffing, cheese, and apple pie.

"It seems like someone was expecting you!" said Alexander in amazement.

"The children! They didn't forget about me, after all!"

Emily was very moved, and Alexander was beside himself with joy. "Oh, look. Food! I'm famished! How marvelous!"

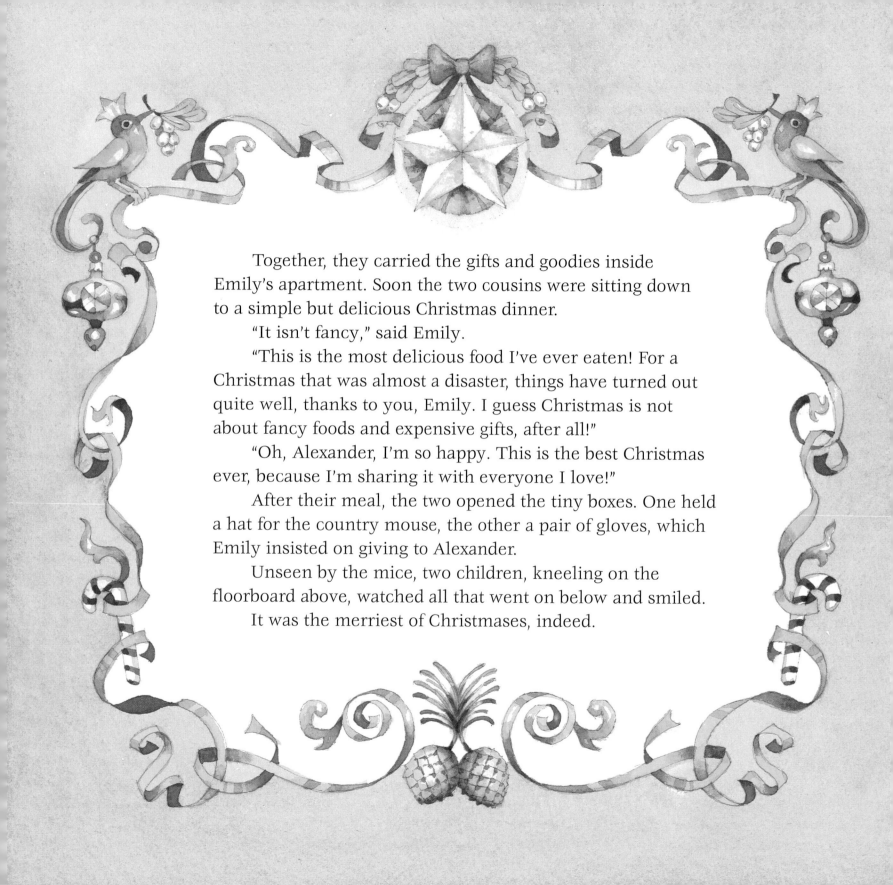

Together, they carried the gifts and goodies inside Emily's apartment. Soon the two cousins were sitting down to a simple but delicious Christmas dinner.

"It isn't fancy," said Emily.

"This is the most delicious food I've ever eaten! For a Christmas that was almost a disaster, things have turned out quite well, thanks to you, Emily. I guess Christmas is not about fancy foods and expensive gifts, after all!"

"Oh, Alexander, I'm so happy. This is the best Christmas ever, because I'm sharing it with everyone I love!"

After their meal, the two opened the tiny boxes. One held a hat for the country mouse, the other a pair of gloves, which Emily insisted on giving to Alexander.

Unseen by the mice, two children, kneeling on the floorboard above, watched all that went on below and smiled.

It was the merriest of Christmases, indeed.